The Sea Chest

Toni Buzzeo ❖ *illustrated by* Mary GrandPré

Dial Books for Young Readers New York

With thanks to the many librarians and historians who assisted me in my historical research: Barbara Skinner Rumsey, Director, Boothbay Regional Historical Society; John R. Clark, Librarian, Boothbay Harbor Memorial Library; Nathan Lipfert, Librarian, Maine Maritime Museum; William David Barry, Historian, Maine Historical Society Research Library; the reference librarians at the Maine State Library and the Portland Public Library, especially Anne Ball and Margo McCain; and with great appreciation to my wonderful editor, Lauri Hornik. This book was made possible, in part, by a Barbara Karlin Grant from the Society of Children's Book Writers and Illustrators. —T.B.

Published by Dial Books for Young Readers
A division of Penguin Putnam Inc.
345 Hudson Street, New York, New York 10014
Text copyright © 2002 by Toni Buzzeo
Illustrations copyright © 2002 by Mary GrandPré
Designed by Mary GrandPré with Atha Tehon
Text set in Bell Monotype
Printed in Hong Kong on acid-free paper
1 3 5 7 9 10 8 6 4 2

Library of Congress Cataloging-in-Publication Data
Buzzeo, Toni.
The sea chest/Toni Buzzeo ; illustrated by Mary GrandPré.
p. cm.
Summary: A young girl listens as her great-great-aunt, a lighthouse keeper's daughter, tells
of her childhood living on a Maine island, and of the infant that washed ashore after a storm.
ISBN 0-8037-2703-8
[1. Rescues—Fiction. 2. Lighthouses—Fiction. 3. Islands—Fiction.
4. Sisters—Fiction. 5. Maine—Fiction.] I. GrandPré, Mary, ill. II. Title.
PZ7.B9832 Se 2002 [Fic]—dc21 2001028255

The art was created with oil paints.

City lights flicker in the dusk
like winking fireflies.
I hold my Auntie Maita's papery hand.
Together we stare at the shiny photo in her lap,
touched so often with hope, the edges curl.
My heartbeat rushes
in an impatient waltz
as we watch for the stranger to arrive.

While we wait,
Auntie Maita remembers her childhood
on a rocky Maine island
eighty years ago and more,
only child of the lighthouse keeper
and his bride.
She gazes out the window
as she tells me the story.

I was a solitary child,
alone on Halleys Head Light
for all my first ten years,
with just my mama
to teach me reading
and just my papa
to spin stories of the boundless world
beyond the rocks of Sanctuary Island.
I longed for a time I might not be
the only child
the craggy island knew.

Spring mornings found me
scrambling beneath the porch,
robbing the brooding hens
of their tawny eggs.
I circled double-yolk days in yellow
on the feed calendar above the davenport.
Supply-boat days were double blue stars,
with their promise of news, fellowship,
and sugar to sweeten summer tea.
When pumpkins burned orange
in the only garden plot
the rocky island held,
first days of home-school
were boxed in red.

But when frost grew thick in winter,
I huddled all day by the fire.
Cloaked in Mama's hand-stitched quilts,
I left the calendar for warmer days
and braided solitary stories.

One icy night,
howling winds blew towering waves
against the shore.
My papa worried
for all the ships upon the sea,
ships in danger of faltering on the rocks
and sinking into the stormy deep.
And when he spotted such a vessel,
out beyond his reach,
Papa could do no more
for the schooner ship nor crew
than burn the light behind the Fresnel lens.

In the frozen dark, the wind shrieked
as wave upon colossal wave
hurled against our rocky shore,
tossing up a churning foam
that battered the parlor windows
and trapped the reflection of firelight
upon the fragile panes.
They rattled and banged until I cried
and prayed they'd not crack in two,
freeing the waves to wash us out to sea.

All the long night,
Mama and I curled up
against that fearsome storm
while Papa made the perilous trip
to and from the square light tower.
We slept not a dream's worth of sleep
through all those blustery hours,
fretting for the ship we could not see.

At dawn, the wind blew itself out
and the storm rolled back
across a glassy sea.
Papa set off to scout the shore
and I went along, as company,
hoping for bits of sea glass
to fill my windowsill jar.
I clung to Papa's hand
in the streaky light
while we slid down
to the farthest rocks.

As we drew near the shore,
we saw a sodden bundle
of eiderdown mattresses
tied with sailor's knots.
It lay heaped upon the rocks,
washed up from the schooner
the storm must have swallowed
in the night.

Our eyes locked wide
when we heard the tiniest cry
from deep inside the padding.
I guessed at a kitten
and held the wish close to my heart.

Squatting beside Papa,
I plucked and pulled with him
at the ragged ends of the icy rope,
our fingers purple without our gloves,
our breath painting clouds of white
in the morning air.

When at last the rope came free,
the mattresses unfolded
to reveal a leather sea chest.
Again I heard the mewl,
and my heart soared with hope
like the gulls reeling overhead,
breaking the morning silence
with their hunger.

Papa lifted the latch and lid,
and I curled my fingers tight.
The frozen hinges squeaked their resistance
then slowly opened wide.

We stared down,
not at a squalling kitten,
but into the face of a small stranger,
more purple than my fingers
from her crying and the cold.
My heart pushed hard against my ribs
as Papa lifted the baby,
wrapped only in a quilt,
into his arms.
My breath caught hard
when he tucked her inside my coat.
My arms enfolded her
as I hummed a cradlesong.

She waved a note
tied to her fragile wrist:

We commit this child
into the hands of God.
May He save her.

-Captain and Mrs. Donald Warren

Papa read the note aloud
and shook his head.
"To think," he said,
"these desperate parents
loved their baby so much,
they were willing to cast her upon the sea."
Tears rolled down my frozen cheeks
as I nestled her close.

There upon the rocks,
I named her Seaborne,
then carried her home
to be my sister.

That sunbright morning,
Mama covered Seaborne's head with kisses
as we held her by the fire,
warming her from without and within.

Through that frosty winter
and on into feathery spring,
alight with purple vetch and yellow buttercup,
my sister slept inside the sea chest
until at last she grew too big.
Then Papa built a trundle
all her own
to tuck beneath my own tall bed.

taught her how to gently probe for eggs
in the dimness under the porch.
We took turns circling double-yolk days,
and made a game
of watching for the supply boat
from the gallery deck.
When the pumpkins ripened on the vine
in sunburnt autumn,
we carried them across the island
and baked pumpkin pies with Mama.

I taught her reading as she grew,
and together we spun stories
of the family living safe and sheltered
above the rocks of Sanctuary Island.

I spent my days,
and all the years of childhood,
with her—your great-grandmother,
and my only sister—Seaborne.
And when I left our island behind
to become a bride,
she soon followed me
to this green mainland,
married, and lived close by
until we buried her last spring,
leaving me an only child again.

*Auntie Maita grows silent,
and now I pause to remember
my great-grandmother's whispery voice,
sharing her stories of two island girls.*

*But my dancing heart can't be still for long.
Tripping wildly,
it beats out a waiting rhythm.
Behind me,
Great-Grandmother Seaborne's
oldest possession,
a cracked and worn sea chest,
lined with an eiderdown quilt,
waits open on the table,
for the tiny stranger
my mama and papa have gone to fetch
from so far across the wide Atlantic.*

To be my sister.

AUTHOR'S NOTE

Although *The Sea Chest* is a fictional story, and Sanctuary Island a fictional island, there is a legend about a severe storm in the Atlantic in the mid-1870's that wrecked a vessel off the coast of Southport Island, Maine. According to the story, the Hendricks Head Light keeper was unable to do anything for the vessel due to the ferocity of the storm. Afterward he found a bundle of feather mattresses washed ashore. Inside was a sea chest holding a baby girl and a note from her parents, the captain and his wife, committing the child into God's hands. The story says that the keeper and his wife had recently lost their own child and that they adopted the baby, named her Seaborne, and raised her as their only child. However, no mention of the child exists in the lighthouse log of the time.

Local historians believe the legend arose from a 1900 C. C. Munn novel entitled *Uncle Terry*. The story was perpetuated in Edward R. Snow's *Famous Lighthouses of New England*.